Pitcher
PRESSURE

BY JAKE MADDOX

illustrated by Sean Tiffany

text by Chris Kreie

STONE ARCH BOOKS

Impact Books are published by Stone Arch Books
151 Good Counsel Drive, P.O. Box 669
Mankato, Minnesota 56002
www.stonearchbooks.com

Library of Congress Cataloging-in-Publication Data
Maddox, Jake.
        Pitcher pressure / by Jake Maddox; text by Chris Kreie;
illustrated by Sean Tiffany.
            p. cm. — (Impact books. A Jake Maddox sports story)
        ISBN 978-1-4342-1596-3
        [1. Baseball—Fiction.] I. Kreie, Chris. II. Tiffany, Sean, ill.
III. Title.
PZ7.M25643Pre 2010
[Fic]—dc22   2009004098

Summary:
Allen's grandpa has never missed a baseball game until tonight. While
Allen plays his most important game ever, Grandpa fights for his life
at the hospital. Allen wants to win the game for his grandpa, but he's
facing his biggest challenge, Hank "The Tank" Steele.

Creative Director: Heather Kindseth
Graphic Designer: Carla Zetina-Yglesias

Table of Contents

CHAPTER 1
The Tank. 5

CHAPTER 2
Time to Pitch 9

CHAPTER 3
Back on Track 16

CHAPTER 4
The Big Blast. 22

CHAPTER 5
A Phone Call 28

CHAPTER 6
News from the Dugout. 34

CHAPTER 7
A Close Play. 41

CHAPTER 8
Hold On to the Victory 47

CHAPTER 9
Stick to the Plan 54

CHAPTER 10
A Message for Grandpa Jim 60

The Tank

CHAPTER 1

Allen dug his shoes into the dirt on the pitcher's mound. He held a baseball behind his back. He rolled the ball around in his fingers and looked at the catcher.

It was the bottom of the second inning of the championship game, and Allen was pitching. The other team, the Tigers, had two outs.

Hank "The Tank" Steele was up to bat. He was on the Tigers.

Everyone called Hank "The Tank" because he was six feet tall and weighed almost 200 pounds. He was the biggest guy in the league. He was also the best player. He was a great hitter.

Allen had already given up a double to The Tank in the first inning. That double had scored two runs for the Tigers. Now Allen's team, the Twins, was losing 3–0.

Allen went into his windup. He kicked his left leg into the air. He reached back with his right hand. Then his entire body shot forward and he let the pitch fly.

The ball sailed into the batter's box and was met by The Tank's bat. Allen turned and watched as the baseball flew high through the air. It flew over the left-field fence for a home run.

The Tank smiled. Then he began his slow jog around the bases. The Tigers fans cheered.

Allen sighed as he looked around the stadium. The sky was pale blue. The sun was hanging low over the fence behind first base. The bleachers were packed with fans who had come to see the Twins and the Tigers battle for the city championship.

It all made Allen think about his Grandpa Jim. It was just the kind of summer evening his grandpa loved.

But that night, as Allen looked into the crowd, he didn't bother looking for his grandpa. Grandpa Jim was not there.

Earlier that day, Grandpa Jim had said his chest hurt. Allen's dad had taken him to the hospital.

Allen wanted to go too, but Grandpa Jim had insisted that it was nothing to worry about. He wasn't going to let Allen miss the championship game. So Allen went to his game while the rest of his family went to the hospital.

The Tank crossed home plate, making the score 4–0. Allen wondered if he had made the right decision after all. He couldn't concentrate on baseball. All he could think about was Grandpa Jim.

Time to Pitch
CHAPTER 2

Allen got the next batter to hit a fly ball to center field. Another player caught it. That was the final out of the second inning.

As he and the Twins ran into the dugout, Allen knew he looked upset. He had given up four runs in just two innings. He wasn't playing like he usually did.

"Shake it off," said his friend Patrick. The two of them took a seat on the dugout bench.

"Don't worry. We'll come back," Patrick added. He slapped Allen on the knee and smiled.

Allen tried to smile back, but he knew his smile didn't look real. Patrick looked concerned.

"How are you doing?" asked Patrick. "Are you going to be okay?"

"I'll be fine," said Allen.

Patrick knew about Allen's grandpa. The whole team knew that Grandpa Jim was in the hospital. Allen had told them about it during warm-ups before the game.

Grandpa Jim was the Twins' biggest fan. Everyone on the team loved him. He was in the stands for every game. He was a friend to all the players. It was weird to play without him watching.

Coach Akers walked over to Allen. "How's it going, Allen?" he asked. "You're a little shaky today. Do you want to stay out there?"

"Yeah, Coach," said Allen. "I want to keep pitching. I think I can do it."

"You think you can do it?" said a voice from the other end of the dugout. It was Thomas, another one of Allen's teammates. Thomas stood up and walked over toward Allen.

"You think you can do it?" Thomas said again. "That's not good enough. You have to know you can do it. This is for the championship."

Allen knew that Thomas was extremely competitive. At one time, he and Allen had been good friends.

That all changed when Allen got the top pitching spot. That had made Thomas mad, and he'd never gotten over it.

"I can pitch, Coach," said Thomas. "I can shut the Tigers down. Allen can't. He's got his grandpa on his mind."

"Really nice, Thomas," said Patrick, shaking his head.

"I make the decisions around here," Coach Akers said. "If Allen says he can pitch, that's all I need to hear."

Thomas stared at Allen and said, "Then you better start pitching like you deserve to be out there. Grandpa Jim wouldn't want the Twins to lose because of you."

Patrick jumped up. He pushed himself between Thomas and Allen. "Back off," said Patrick. "Don't say another word."

"Take it easy, guys," said Coach Akers.

"It's okay," said Allen. He stood up. "It's okay. Thomas is right."

"What?" said Patrick. He looked at Allen and frowned.

"He's right," said Allen. "Grandpa wouldn't want me to lose the game. He wouldn't like it if I lost the championship because I was worrying about him. Thomas is right. If I can't concentrate on the game, I shouldn't be out there."

"I'm glad you can admit that," said Thomas. He turned to Coach Akers and asked, "So, do you want me to pitch?"

"No," said Allen. "I didn't say that. I can concentrate. We will win. I'm staying in the game. I can do it."

"Great," said Coach Akers, walking away.

"Then you better start pitching," said Thomas. He walked back to his spot at the other end of the dugout. "You better shut 'em down."

Allen and Patrick sat back down. "Don't listen to him," said Patrick.

"But he's right," said Allen. "It's time for me to forget about my grandpa and just go out and pitch. The team deserves it."

"All right then," said Patrick. He grinned at Allen. "Let's do it."

Allen smiled back. "Let's do it," he said.

Back on Track
CHAPTER 3

Allen stood on the pitcher's mound to start the third inning. The score was still 4–0. The Twins still hadn't scored a run. It was more important than ever for Allen to get back on track and shut down the Tigers.

Allen kicked at the dirt. Then he went into his windup. He gunned the pitch toward home. It was a perfect pitch, right on the outside corner of the plate. The batter couldn't get it. He watched it sail by.

"Strike!" yelled the umpire.

"Great job, Allen!" shouted Patrick from his spot at third base.

Allen stayed focused as he got the ball back from the catcher. He moved the baseball from his glove hand into his throwing hand.

He stared toward home. Then he reached back and threw another hard pitch toward the batter.

This time the batter swung, but he was slow getting the bat through the hitting zone. He fouled it off down the right-field line.

Strike two!

Allen took a deep breath. He hadn't had a strikeout all game. This would be the perfect time for one.

He spun the baseball in his fingers and went into his windup. Then he kicked his leg forward and uncorked a fastball toward home.

The batter stepped into the pitch. He swung hard. The ball landed in the catcher's glove.

Strike three!

"Yeah!" shouted Patrick. "That's it! The strikeout king is back."

Coach Akers was standing up in the dugout, clapping. The crowd was cheering. Allen nodded and smiled.

He felt good. He knew it was just one strikeout, but it still felt really good.

Allen pitched to the next batter. He got another strikeout.

Then, after two perfect pitches to the third batter for two more strikes, Allen paused for just an instant. He thought about Grandpa Jim.

This one's for you, Grandpa, Allen thought. *This one's for all you've done for me.*

It was his grandpa, after all, who had taught Allen how to pitch. Grandpa Jim had stayed in the backyard for hours, helping to make Allen's fastball perfect.

As Allen went into his windup, he knew that Grandpa Jim wasn't there. Grandpa Jim was sitting in some hospital room. But for some reason, Allen felt like one good pitch, one good fastball in just the right place, would help his grandpa.

It was the only way Allen could help. He could strike out three batters in a row.

Somehow, that energy would reach his grandpa in the hospital. Somehow.

Allen let the pitch fly. He watched it sail into the batter's box. The batter watched it too. The ball flew perfectly across the plate and into the catcher's glove. *Thud!*

"Strike!" yelled the umpire. The crowd, and all of Allen's teammates, jumped to their feet.

"Yes," said Allen quietly to himself. He smiled and added, "Hope that helps, Grandpa."

The Big Blast
CHAPTER 4

The other Twins players crowded around Allen as he took a seat in the dugout. They all patted him on the shoulders and congratulated him on the three strikeouts in a row.

"Quit celebrating," said Thomas, frowning. "We're still down by four runs."

"Okay, guys," said Coach Akers. "Let's get some runs back. Allen, you're up!"

It was the top of the fourth inning. In all the excitement of the strikeouts, Allen had forgotten that it was going to be his turn to bat next.

Allen grabbed his bat and helmet and walked toward home plate. In the batter's box he adjusted his helmet and tried to concentrate on hitting. It was always difficult for him to hit in the games when he pitched, since he put so much focus into pitching.

Just get on base, Allen told himself as he stood in the batter's box. *Just get on base and Thomas will drive me home.*

Thomas was up next, and he was a great hitter. If Allen got on base, Thomas could drive him home with the first Twins run of the game.

The Tigers pitcher went into his windup and threw the ball. Allen waited for just an instant, and then quickly swung the bat.

He hit the ball hard. It shot toward the shortstop between second base and third base. Allen dug his feet into the dirt and sprinted toward first base.

The shortstop scooped up the ball. Allen ran fast. He knew it would be a long throw to the first basemen.

Allen's foot touched the base. Then, half a second later, the ball landed in the first baseman's glove.

"Safe!" shouted the umpire.

Allen's heart pumped hard as he caught his breath. He smiled. He had done just what he had wanted to do. He had gotten on base.

Thomas took his spot in the batter's box. Allen carefully stepped off first base for a short lead.

The next pitch floated right over the heart of the plate. Thomas swung his bat into it. He blasted the ball far into the outfield and over the center-field fence for a home run.

Allen raced around the bases. Then, out of breath, he waited at home for Thomas to join him.

The crowd was going nuts. The players in the Twins dugout were giving each other high fives.

Thomas rounded third base. Then he jogged into home.

Allen held his hand high above his head. "Great hit, man," he told Thomas.

Thomas slapped his hand. "Now shut down those Tigers," Thomas said.

"I'm on it," said Allen. The two ran back to their cheering teammates in the dugout.

A Phone Call

CHAPTER 5

Allen stood on the pitcher's mound. He remembered the day he'd asked his grandpa to teach him how to throw a curve ball. His grandpa had said he should keep working on his fastball, since he could hurt his arm pitching a curve ball.

"Besides," Grandpa had said, "the best pitchers in the major leagues use their fastballs most of the time. And you have a major-league fastball."

"Batter up!" yelled the umpire.

The umpire's voice yanked Allen out of his daydream.

"Here we go, Allen," Patrick shouted from third base. "Just one more batter!"

The Twins were still behind, but only by one run. Thanks to Thomas's home run in the fourth inning and another Twins run in the top of the sixth, Allen's team was only down 4–3.

It was the bottom of the sixth inning. There were two outs. Allen had gotten the first two batters out that inning by pitching the way his grandpa had always taught him.

He had learned to keep the fastball low in the strike zone. Move it around. Try to put the ball across the corners of the plate.

Allen took one last second to think about his grandpa. Then he fired a pitch across the plate, right at the batter's knees.

"Strike!" yelled the umpire.

Keep us in the game, thought Allen. *Just get the batter out.*

"You can do it, Allen!" shouted Patrick. "Another one just like that!"

Allen got the ball back and went into his windup. *Low on the outside corner*, he thought to himself as he let the ball go.

The ball cruised low through the strike zone on the outside part of home plate. It was exactly the pitch he wanted to throw. The batter took a mighty swing, but hit nothing but air.

Strike two!

Allen got the ball back from the catcher. He took a deep breath, trying to stay relaxed.

As Allen got prepared to pitch, he glanced toward the dugout. He expected to see Coach Akers on the top step of the dugout, giving him encouragement. But what he saw surprised him.

Coach Akers wasn't standing on the top step. In fact, he wasn't even standing. He was sitting inside the dugout, talking on his cell phone.

Coach never talks on the phone during games, Allen thought. *Could it be news from the hospital?*

Allen stepped off the mound. He felt himself starting to sweat. *Pull yourself together,* he thought. *It's probably nothing.*

He took one more deep breath. Then he got back onto the mound and set his feet in the dirt. He went into his motion, and then gunned the ball toward home.

The batter swung and missed again. "Strike!" yelled the umpire.

Allen didn't even hear the cheers as he raced into the dugout.

News from the *Dugout*
CHAPTER 6

Coach Akers clicked his phone shut just as Allen sprinted down the dugout steps.

"Coach, who were you talking to?" asked Allen, out of breath.

Coach Akers put his hand on Allen's shoulder. "I think you should sit down," Coach said.

Allen frowned. "I'm not sitting down," he said. He knew he shouldn't talk to his coach that way, but he was upset.

Allen stepped forward and raised his voice. "Just tell me," he said. "Who were you talking to?"

The other players looked at him. They all looked worried.

Patrick walked over. "Allen, is everything all right?" he asked.

"Patrick, this is private," said Coach Akers.

"It's okay. Patrick can hear," said Allen. His anger and fear were building. "I just want to know what you found out."

"It's your grandpa," said Coach Akers.

Allen felt a wave of panic rush over him. He asked, "Is he okay?"

"Well, they think he will be okay," said Coach Akers.

"What's going on?" Allen asked.

Coach Akers said, "Your grandpa had a heart attack."

This can't be happening, Allen thought. *This can't be real.*

"That was your dad on the phone," said Coach Akers. "He said that your grandpa is going to have an emergency procedure. But he also said that if everything goes as planned, Grandpa Jim should be just fine."

"Just give me a minute," said Allen. He sat down on the bench and pulled his cap over his eyes.

Memories of Grandpa Jim poured into his brain. Allen fought back tears.

What if I never see him again? he thought to himself. *People die every day from heart attacks.*

Coach Akers put his hand on Allen's shoulder. "I think we should pull you out of the game," Coach said. "Your dad could come right over and pick you up. You could be there when your grandpa gets out of the operating room."

"I don't know," Allen said quietly. "I can't think straight."

"It would be okay," said Patrick. "The team would understand."

"What would be okay?" asked Thomas, marching over from his spot in the dugout.

"None of your business," said Patrick.

"No, Patrick, it's okay," said Allen. He looked at Thomas. "My grandpa had a heart attack," Allen told him.

"No way," said Thomas. "You're kidding, right?"

"No, he's not," said Patrick. "Why do you think Allen's been so worried the whole game? You knew his grandpa was sick."

"I didn't think it was that serious," said Thomas. "I'm sorry. I had no idea."

"Allen, I'll give you a few minutes to think it over," said Coach Akers. "You can do whatever you'd like."

"He doesn't need a few minutes," said Thomas. "He's staying in. He has to stay in. We need him. We need him to stay in and win this thing for us and for Grandpa Jim."

"Thanks, Thomas," said Allen. "Coach, I agree with Thomas. I'm staying in."

"Are you sure?" asked Coach Akers.

"I'm sure," said Allen. "That's what Grandpa Jim would want me to do."

"That's what I like to hear," said Thomas.

"The strikeout king isn't done yet," said Patrick.

The three teammates raised their fists in the air and pounded them together.

"Let's go beat those Tigers!" said Allen.

A Close Play

CHAPTER 7

Allen prepared to bat in the top of the seventh inning. It was the last inning of the game. The Twins were still behind 4–3. If Allen and the Twins wanted to win, they would need at least two runs.

Patrick grabbed a bat and a helmet. He was first up. Allen took his place on deck, since he was batting next.

"Drive the ball!" yelled Thomas from the dugout.

Patrick let the first pitch go outside for a ball. Then he swung at — and missed — the next pitch.

"You can do it!" shouted Allen.

Patrick dug his feet into the dirt around home plate. The pitch sailed toward him. Patrick swung hard and connected. The ball flew through the infield and past the second baseman for a solid hit.

"That's it!" shouted Allen.

He walked toward home plate. He stepped into the batter's box. He felt calm. He breathed easily and his heart beat normally.

He wasn't nervous about baseball anymore. He felt good as he looked out at the pitcher. Somehow, he just knew he was going to get a hit.

The first pitch flew toward him. Allen drove it toward the outfield. It bounced in front of the left fielder for a hit. Allen ran to first base. Patrick ran to second.

"You ripped that thing!" yelled Patrick.

Allen looked toward home plate. "Thomas, drive us in!" he shouted.

Thomas walked toward the plate. The pitcher wound up.

Allen took a two-step lead off first base. He wanted to be ready to run.

The sky was beginning to darken. Soon the stadium lights would go on. Grandpa Jim loved nights like this. If the Twins came back to win and if Grandpa was okay, Allen would have a great story to tell him.

The pitcher went into his windup. The ball flew toward home plate.

Thomas kicked his front leg off the ground and thrust his entire body forward. His bat met the ball and drove a hit deep into the outfield.

Allen sprinted toward second. As he ran, he watched the ball bounce past the center fielder and roll all the way toward the fence. In front of him, Patrick rounded third and easily made it home.

As Allen approached third base, he looked at the dugout. Coach Akers was giving him the signal to run home.

Allen raced around third and sprinted for home. Patrick was waving both of his arms toward the ground. That meant it was going to be a close play.

Allen knew what the signal meant. Patrick was telling him to slide.

Just as the ball reached the catcher, Allen dove into home plate. His left hand crossed the plate an instant before the catcher tagged him.

"Safe!" yelled the umpire.

Allen and Patrick jumped up and down, cheering. Then they looked at Thomas. He was standing on second base, smiling.

The score was 5–4. The Twins were finally ahead.

Hold On to the Victory
CHAPTER 8

At the bottom of the seventh inning, the score was still 5–4. After Thomas's blast, the Tigers had gotten the next three Twins on easy outs.

The Twins were ahead, but only by one run. It was up to Allen to keep the Tigers from scoring.

It was the last inning of the game. Allen had to hold on to the victory. He had to keep the Twins in the lead.

Allen grabbed his glove and headed out to the pitcher's mound. As he was crossing the infield, the stadium lights suddenly blasted on.

Under the powerful white lights, the grass seemed greener. The bases seemed to shine. "Baseball under the lights," his grandpa always said. "Nothing's better."

Allen agreed. Summer baseball under the lights was what he lived for.

Allen stepped onto the mound. He took one long, deep breath. *Keep pitching your game*, he thought to himself. *Nothing fancy. Just three easy outs.*

"End this thing!" shouted Thomas.

"Let's get 'em!" shouted Patrick from third base. "Put 'em down, right in a row, 1-2-3!"

Allen knew Patrick was right. If he could get the first three batters out, if he could get the Tigers out fast, his job would be much easier.

Hank the Tank was supposed to bat fifth. If Allen could get the first three batters out, he wouldn't have to worry about facing The Tank.

Allen took one last big breath. Then he got ready to pitch.

After Allen looked in at the catcher, he went into his windup. Then he threw the first pitch of the inning.

The batter swung and connected, but it was just a simple ground ball to second base. The second baseman picked up the ball and tossed it to first.

One out!

Two outs to go, thought Allen.

"Yes!" shouted Patrick. "Two more, just like that!"

Allen got back up on the pitching mound. He waited for the next batter to step onto home plate.

Allen kept his eyes focused on the catcher's glove. He knew that the fans were on their feet. They were going wild. But Allen couldn't get distracted. He kept his eyes glued on the catcher.

Allen went into his windup. He fired another pitch toward home plate. Again, the batter swung, and again, the bat met the ball.

The ball sailed into the air toward third base. Patrick took a couple steps back and waited. The ball fell easily into his glove.

Two outs!

Only one more, thought Allen. *Then we win the championship.*

Patrick jogged toward Allen. "One more out, man," Patrick said. "Let's win this thing." He placed the ball in Allen's glove and jogged back to third base.

This is almost too easy, thought Allen. *I made two pitches and we got two easy outs.*

Grandpa Jim had always told him that getting the last out was the hardest. There was no time to relax.

Allen kicked some dirt around the mound. Then he looked at the catcher. He went into his windup. Then he threw a hard fastball toward home.

The batter swung and missed.

Strike one!

Allen's next pitch missed the plate for a ball. The one after that hit the inside corner for another strike.

One more strike and it's over, thought Allen. *I can do it.*

He rolled the ball in his fingers. Then he went into his pitching motion. The ball flew into the batter's box. The batter swung. His bat connected with the ball, sending a solid base hit into the outfield. The batter ran to first base. The center fielder threw the ball to the infield.

Allen knew that Grandpa Jim had been right. The last out never was easy.

As the next batter set himself in the batter's box, Allen waited. He turned to look at the runner on first.

Allen kicked his front leg into the air and let the pitch fly. The batter stepped into the pitch and blasted a hit to right field. Allen watched as the runner on first rounded second base and made it to third.

The outfielder returned the ball to Allen. He looked at home plate. Then he felt a sick, nervous feeling in his stomach.

The player stepping into the batter's box was Hank "The Tank" Steele.

Stick to the Plan

Patrick jogged to the pitcher's mound. "You can get this guy," he told Allen. "I know it and you know it. Just stick to your game plan and get him out."

"Got it," said Allen. "Nothing fancy. Just get him out."

The Tank was the best hitter in the league. If Allen wanted to get him out, he knew Patrick was right. He needed to stick to the plan.

He'd throw The Tank low pitches. He'd change speeds and try to hit the corners. That's what Grandpa had taught him.

"Batter up!" yelled the umpire.

Allen took a breath. He focused all his energy on home plate. The crowd, the lights, the green grass — none of those things mattered. All that mattered was striking out The Tank.

Allen went into his windup. The ball left his hand and shot toward home plate. Hank watched as the ball flew past him.

"Strike!" said the umpire.

Hank stepped out of the batter's box and stared at Allen. Allen got the ball from the catcher and immediately got back on the pitcher's mound. He wanted to end the game quickly.

Allen looked toward home. Then he went into his pitching motion. He threw the ball hard. He wanted to blow the pitch right by The Tank. He knew The Tank wouldn't just watch two good pitches.

The pitch rocketed toward home, and The Tank was all over it. He brought his bat quickly through the hitting zone and totally crushed the ball. It was power against power, and Hank's bat won.

Allen watched as the ball flew through the sky. It was like a missile. It kept going up and up and up. The umpire ran toward third base. He watched carefully as the ball flew over the outfield fence.

"Foul ball!" yelled the umpire.

Allen let out a deep breath. *That was way too close,* he thought.

Hank "The Tank" Steele jogged back to home plate and picked up his bat.

"Just one more strike," Patrick yelled.

"You can do it!" Thomas said.

Hank Steele had just smashed Allen's last pitch. It was almost a game-winning home run. But it was still strike two. Allen needed just one more strike for the championship.

Allen could hear the voice of Grandpa Jim in his head. "Power hitters want you to throw hard every pitch," Grandpa had said. "They like the hard stuff. Keep them off balance. Change speeds."

As he took a deep breath, Allen looked toward the sky. "This is it, Grandpa," he said out loud. "This one is for the championship."

Allen pulled the ball behind his body. Then he stepped toward the plate and let the ball go.

Change speeds, he thought. *Change speeds.*

The ball practically floated as it slowly soared toward home plate. The crowd got silent as they watched the ball head toward Hank "The Tank" Steele.

The Tank couldn't resist the pitch. He stepped toward the ball and swung with everything he had.

Thud! The ball landed in the catcher's glove. Hank had swung too hard and missed the ball by a mile.

Strike three! The game was over.

A Message for
Grandpa Jim

The entire Twins team ran to the pitching mound. Patrick was the first player to get there.

"You did it, man!" yelled Patrick. He grabbed Allen in a tight hug. "You did it!"

"No, we did it!" shouted Allen.

Thomas ran in. "You struck out Hank 'The Tank' Steele," he yelled. "Unbelievable."

As his teammates celebrated in the middle of the field, Allen looked out at the crowd. *Grandpa should be here,* he thought. *I wish he was here to see this.*

Patrick stepped in front of Allen. "You'll just have to tell him about it," he said.

"What?" Allen asked, confused.

"Grandpa Jim," said Patrick. "You'll just have to tell him about the game when you see him later."

"How did you know that's what I was thinking?" asked Allen.

"We're best friends," said Patrick. "Don't you know that I can read your mind?"

"Thanks, man," said Allen, smiling.

Allen looked around at the players and fans on the field. Someone was missing.

"Hey, Patrick," Allen said. "Where's Coach?"

Patrick looked around the field. "There," he said, pointing into the dugout.

Coach Akers was sitting on the bench, holding a cell phone to his ear.

"Let's go," said Patrick.

"Okay," Allen said nervously. He and Patrick jogged to the dugout.

When they arrived, Coach Akers stood up and put the phone in his back pocket. He smiled.

"Good news, Allen," Coach said. "That was your dad. Your grandpa came through his procedure just fine. He's going to be okay. Your dad is on his way right now to pick you up."

"Yes!" shouted Patrick. "I knew he would be okay. Your grandpa is no quitter."

Allen smiled. He felt a huge sense of relief. His grandpa was fine, and his team just won the championship. It was time to celebrate.

"Go out there and get your medals," said Coach Akers.

Allen and Patrick jogged back onto the field. They joined the rest of the Twins players in a line.

After a few minutes, a league official walked down the line. He gave the players championship medals as their names were announced over a loudspeaker.

Allen heard his name over the speakers. He shook the official's hand and received his medal.

He stood in the middle of the field, on the green grass. Under the bright lights, he whispered a message. "Grandpa Jim," he said. "I've got a great story for you."

About the Author

Chris Kreie lives in Minnesota with his wife and two children. He works as a school librarian, and in his free time he writes books like this. Some of his other books in this series include *Gridiron Bully* and *Wild Hike*.

About the Illustrator

When Sean Tiffany was growing up, he lived on a small island off the coast of Maine. Every day, from sixth grade until he graduated from high school, he had to take a boat to get to school. When Sean isn't working on his art, he works on a multimedia project called "OilCan Drive," which combines music and art. He has a pet cactus named Jim.

Glossary

approached (uh-PROHCHD)—got nearer

championship (CHAM-pee-uhn-ship)—the final game of a series that determines which team or player will be the overall winner

competitive (kuhm-PET-uh-tiv)—very eager to win

concentrate (KON-suhn-trate)—to focus your thoughts and attention on something

congratulated (kuhn-GRACH-uh-late-id)—told someone that you were pleased that he or she did something well

emergency (i-MUR-juhn-see)—sudden and dangerous

encouragement (en-KUR-ij-muhnt)—support or praise given to someone

energy (EN-ur-jee)—the strength to do active things without getting tired

procedure (pruh-SEE-jur)—a medical test or operation

More About
Famous Pitchers

More pitchers have been inducted into the Baseball Hall of Fame than any other baseball position. Here are just a few of them.

Sandy Koufax played for the the Dodgers from 1955–1966. In 1965, the Dodgers were playing the Minnesota Twins in the World Series. The first game of the series fell on the Jewish holiday Yom Kippur. Koufax refused to play that day. He did pitch in other games of the series, which the Los Angeles Dodgers won, 4 games to 3.

Cy Young's first season in the MLB was 1890. In 1903, he helped the Boston Americans win the first-ever World Series. Young pitched the first American League perfect game on May 5, 1904, against the Philadelphia Athletics.

Whitey Ford spent all 18 years of his baseball career playing for the New York Yankees. He was voted the American League's Rookie of the Year in 1950. But during 1951 and 1952, Ford served in the Army during the Korean War. In 1953, he returned to the New York Yankees. He won 236 games for the Yankees, the most games won by any Yankees pitcher. In 1974, the Yankees retired his number, 16.

Nolan Ryan played major league baseball for 27 seasons (more than any other player). Ryan is most famous for his incredibly fast pitches — some of them were recorded over 100 miles per hour. That's almost twice as fast as a car traveling on a highway!

Discussion Questions

1. Allen and Thomas used to be close friends, but at the beginning of this book, they aren't friends anymore. Why not?

2. Allen's friends on the team know that he's upset about his grandpa. What are some things you can do to help a friend who's upset?

3. Allen is nervous about striking out Hank "The Tank" Steele. When you're nervous, what can you do to calm down?

Writing Prompts

1. In this book, Allen is very close to his grandpa. Choose one of your grandparents to write about. Include details like where and when your grandparent was born, what he or she did/does for a living, and what kind of hobbies he or she had/has.

2. What do you think happens after this book ends? Write another chapter that picks up where this book leaves off!

3. Allen gets support from his friends and teammates in this book. Write about someone who gives you support. How does that person help you?